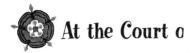
At the Court o

Essex
Wants it All

by Karen Wallace
Illustrated by Jane Cope

W
FRANKLIN WATTS
LONDON•SYDNEY

First published in 2001 by
Franklin Watts
96 Leonard Street
London EC2A 4XD

Franklin Watts Australia
56 O'Riordan Street
Alexandria
NSW 2015

Editor: Louise John
Designer: Jason Anscomb
Consultant: Dr Anne Millard, BA Hons, Dip Ed, PhD

A CIP catalogue record for this book
is available from the British Library.

ISBN   0 7496 4073 1 (hbk)
        0 7496 4373 0 (pbk)

Dewey Classification 942.05

Printed in Great Britain

To Louise, with thanks. K

At the Court of Queen Elizabeth

Essex
Wants it All

by Karen Wallace
Illustrated by Jane Cope

W
FRANKLIN WATTS
LONDON•SYDNEY

The Characters

Mary Marchbank

Earl of Essex

Matilda, Lady Mouthwater

Queen Elizabeth

Toby Crumble

Earl Inkblot

Old Ma Knucklebone

Lord Roderick Crusty

CONTENTS

🏵 CHAPTER ONE 🏵
A Charming Present

The Earl of Essex put on his most ravishing smile and made his dark eyes twinkle. He leaned forward, as graceful as a swan, on his bended knee.

"Most heavenly daughter of the moon! Most beauteous spirit of the dawn. Most lovely sovereign of my heart!"

In front of him, Queen Elizabeth I tittered and rearranged the huge red wig that rose like a sail above her head. Two long ringlets fell on either side of her yellow, papery face.

The Queen smiled to herself. She was sure she looked more like sixteen than sixty-three. And she was sure the Earl of Essex, who was barely into his twenties, thought so, too.

"My Sweet Essex," murmured the Queen. She held out a knobbly hand for him to kiss. "What is it that you want?"

Essex pressed his lips against the Queen's fingers. "Me? Your Majesty, I want for nothing in your presence."

He reached into a long, leather pouch that hung from his belt. "Indeed, I have brought you a present," he murmured seductively and handed over a beautifully wrapped narrow box.

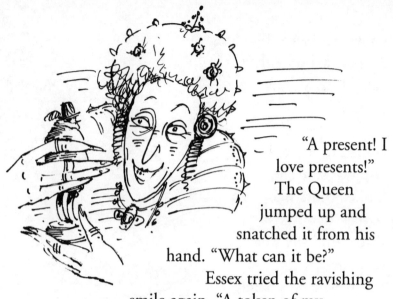

"A present! I love presents!" The Queen jumped up and snatched it from his hand. "What can it be?"

Essex tried the ravishing smile again. "A token of my affection," he murmured.

The Queen ripped away the wrapping and stared at the small figurine in her hand. "Why, it's a statue of you!" she cried. "How wonderful!"

"So that I will be with you always, Your Majesty," replied the Earl of Essex smoothly.

A girlish blush spread across the Queen's cheeks, turning her yellow skin a curious orange colour.

"And I, you, Lord Essex," cried the Queen, looking up through her pale, stubby eyelashes, "were it not for my other duties, of course."

Essex saw his chance. "Ah, duties," he jumped in. "Indeed, duties are of much interest to me!"

8

The Queen leaned forward and pinched his cheek. "Duties on sweet wines, by any chance?" She sat back and chortled. "I seem to remember you spoke of them at our last meeting."

"Your Majesty has a memory like the noble beast of the Indes," replied Essex, his voice as smooth as toffee.

"Indeed I do," cried the Queen. "And I also remember another of your desires." She clapped her hands as if she was very pleased with herself. "The position of Gentleman of the Horse in my household."

The Earl of Essex made his eyes twinkle brighter than ever and he kissed the Queen's hand once again.

Across the other side of chamber, Godfrey ,Earl of Inkblot, coughed loudly. Roderick, Lord Crusty, sniffed noisily.

Beside them, Matilda, Lady Mouthwater, snapped the long narrow paint brush she was holding and glared at the Earl of Essex with eyes like dagger points.

Even Mary Marchbank, who always tried to think the best of everyone, turned to hide the angry line of her mouth.

Only last week, the Queen had given the right to charge taxes and duties on sweet wines to the Earl of Inkblot in recognition for his dedication and work.

She had appointed Roderick, Lord Crusty, Gentleman of the Horse in her household, in return for his long and loyal service.

Now this flattering, lying troublemaker was stealing them for himself.

SNAP!

Matilda, Lady Mouthwater, broke another paintbrush. Mary stared at her. She knew only too well that poor Lady Mouthwater had spent every day since the Earl of Essex had arrived back at court, trying to avoid his pesky attentions.

Indeed Mary had even heard Lady Mouthwater, who was usually so quiet and shy, shout, "Get lost, Goat Face! I don't even like you."

But Essex had merely stroked his beard and smiled. "So what? The Queen does."

As for Mary herself, she had no reason to feel any loyalty towards the Earl of Essex either. Quite the opposite. He had commissioned her sweetheart,

Sydney Woodshavings, who was Furniture Maker to the Queen, to make a huge oak chair. In fact, Sydney had said it was more like a throne than a chair. And even though Sydney had made a lovely job of it, when it came to paying for it, Essex had claimed he didn't have a penny to his name.

Mary felt her own cheeks flush with anger. How could she and Sydney save up to get married if noblemen like Essex refused to pay what they owed?

"For the love of sweetmeats!" cried the Queen, suddenly seeing the faces of her servants across the chamber. "Why the dark faces?"

She patted the Earl's cheek. "See, my dear, what dullards and imbeciles I am surrounded by!"

Godfrey, Earl Inkblot, took a deep breath. His face was indeed dark purple with rage. "Your Majesty," he choked, "on the matter of sweet wines –"

"And as your Gentleman of the Horse," interrupted Lord Roderick, almost in tears.

The Queen's eyes flashed menacingly.

"The matter is closed, Sir Godfrey," she yelped. "And Lord Roderick, I have changed my mind!"

The Earl of Essex turned to where the others were standing. He picked up a pack of cards and fanned them in front of his face.

His ravishing smile had turned into a smug smirk and his dark brown eyes were as hard and shiny as bullets.

TUDOR FURNITURE FOR EVERY OCCASION

14

❀ CHAPTER TWO ❀
A Clever Plan

Mary Marchbank never thought she would see the day when Godfrey, Earl of Inkblot, and Roderick, Lord Crusty, would be so interested in talking to each other. She poured out mugs of mead and set them on the table between the two men.

For the first time ever, Lord Crusty and the Earl of Inkblot had something very important in common.

As indeed, they all did. Which was why Godfrey,

Earl Inkblot had called a meeting in his chambers to see what could be done about the Earl of Essex.

Matilda, Lady Mouthwater crossed the long chamber and sat down at the table.

"I'll have a mug too, please, Mary."

Mary was so astonished, her mouth dropped open.

It was unheard of for Lady Mouthwater to have more than a sip of elderflower cordial!

She put another mug on the table and half-filled it with mead.

"Up to the top," muttered Godfrey, Earl of Inkblot. "We need all the help we can get here."

Matilda, Lady Mouthwater, downed her mead in one, and wiped her mouth on her sleeve – she obviously meant business. "So what are we going to do?" she demanded.

Roderick, Lord Crusty, took a sip of his mead. It was warm and strong and went straight to his head. "I think we should make twouble for the twouble-maker," he giggled.

"Good idea, Roderick," said Godfrey, Earl Inkblot, raising his eyebrows to the ceiling. "But how?"

Lord Roderick took another sip of mead. "Get him into twouble, of course."

"What kind of trouble, Roderick?" asked Godfrey, patiently.

Lord Crusty took yet another sip. "Sewious twouble," he muttered, looking as fierce as he could.

Mary watched nervously as the Earl of Inkblot rolled his eyes and made a strange grinding noise with his teeth.

Matilda, Lady Mouthwater drained another mug and

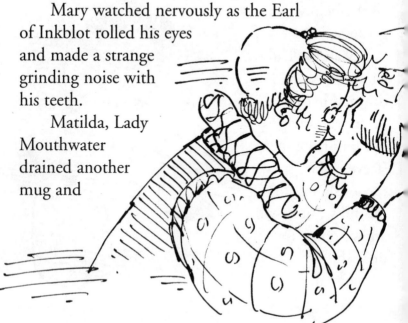

held it out for her third refill. "Thing is," she said slowly. "He's a cunning fox so, whatever we do, he mustn't suspect anything."

The three of them looked at each other. The truth was that none of them was clever enough to out-fox the Earl of Essex.

Suddenly Roderick, Lord Crusty, pulled out a big handkerchief and began to sniff noisily.

"I'd told everyone about being appointed Gentleman of the Horse," he wailed. "Even my mother!"

"And I'd started building my own manor house with the wine duties," howled Godfrey, Earl Inkblot. "Now I'll never be able to finish it."

Matilda, Lady Mouthwater, slammed her mug down on the table. "I HATE him!" she shouted at the top of her voice. "I wish he was DEAD!"

Nobody spoke.

Lord Roderick blew his nose.

"I've got an idea," said Mary Marchbank in a quiet voice. "It's, um, rather odd, but it might just work."

Three pairs of red-rimmed eyes stared at her, hopefully.

Mary swallowed. "Let's ask Old Ma –"

"Oh, no!" cried Godfrey, Earl Inkblot, before Mary could finish. He put his hands over his face and shook his head. "I can't bear it. She's just soooo smelly."

Mary bit her lip. The Earl was right. The last time she had visited Old Ma Knucklebone's hovel, she'd had to throw away the clothes she was wearing.

And it was no good asking Old Ma Knucklebone to come to visit you, because any room she occupied for more than five seconds was just never the same again, no matter how many

bunches of dried lavender you burned to get rid of the lingering smell.

"What if we meet her in the stables?" suggested Mary. "There must be somewhere there that is fairly smelly already."

Godfrey, Earl Inkblot, looked up quickly. "There is a tiny room right at the end! No one uses it."

"I do!" cried Roderick Crusty in a hurt voice. "That little woom is beside my LusciousLizzie's stable and it's as sweet-smelling as a meadow of daisies."

"Not for much longer," muttered Godfrey, Earl Inkblot.

He scribbled a picture on a note, stamped it with his seal and handed it to Mary. "Get this to Old Ma Knucklebone right away, Mary!" he cried.

***

Old Ma Knucklebone stared at the note.

She couldn't read, of course. But she knew what a stable looked like and she recognised the seal.

Godfrey, Earl of Inkblot!

Old Ma Knucklebone sighed. There was a time when she would have done anything for him.

And he for her.

Mind you, that was after she had swallowed some of her own love potion by mistake and then tricked him into swallowing some, too.

Old Ma Knucklebone sighed again. It had been a brief but passionate affair.

Brief because the potion didn't last long. And passionate because when Sir Godfrey had discovered the reason behind his strange behaviour, he had almost exploded with rage.

Old Ma Knucklebone pulled on her greasy cap with the lucky foxtail hanging down the back and felt for the small bag of bones she always wore at her belt.

Now the dear boy needed her again. Well, she was not a lady to bear a grudge!

Old Ma Knucklebone smeared some green ointment behind her ears and breathed in the sweet smell of swamp. Grinning to herself, she set off for her secret meeting at the stables.

CHAPTER THREE
A Secret Meeting

Roderick, Lord Crusty, hadn't taken any chances. In every corner of the stable room, a small incense burner smouldered. Huge bunches of sweet-smelling herbs hung from hooks around the walls.

He had even filled lockets with rose petals and handed them out for his visitors to wear.

Because the truth was that Roderick spent most of his time in this little room at the end of the stables. And the last thing he wanted was Old Ma Knucklebone to stink it out.

Now, as he watched the filthy old hag hitch up her grey skirts, dig under her crusted yellow apron and flop her leather pouch on top of an old beer barrel, his nose twitched and his heart sank.

The foul smell of swamp rose like a dank mist to fill the room. Any trace of incense or herbs or rose petals had already vanished.

"I can tell you're all pleased to see me." Old Ma Knucklebone threw back her head and cackled. "Green's my favourite colour!"

Mary Marchbank looked at Earl Inkblot, Lady Mouthwater and Lord Roderick. Their faces were three different shades of green!

"Um, it was very kind of you to come," whispered Mary, knowing that her face must be green too and hoping against hope that she wouldn't be sick.

"I always comes when I'm needed, dearie," replied Old Ma Knucklebone. As she spoke, she emptied out her pouch and sent a handful of grimy bones rolling over the barrel top.

"Now let's see what we can do about that Earl of Essex."

Earl Inkblot made a noise like a camel choking. How did the old hag know that was why they had summoned her?

"I just does, dearie." Old Ma Knucklebone grinned, reading his mind.

And everyone in the room knew she was right! Old Ma Knucklebone had saved the day many times.

Godfrey, Earl Inklbot, tried to hold his nose and speak at the same time. "What do you see, mistress?" he asked, gulping for air.

"A party," replied Old Ma Knucklebone.

"What kind of party?" croaked Matilda, Lady Mouthwater, holding a perfumed handkerchief to her face.

Old Ma Knucklebone thrust her whiskery face forward. She looked just like a bloated squirrel.

"A birthday party," she breathed. "A birthday party with lots of presents."

"Any particular kind of presents?" gasped Lord Roderick Crusty, staggering forward and falling into a chair.

Old Ma Knucklebone nodded

"If my plan is to work," she said in a serious voice. "Everyone must give the Earl something he would use on the battlefield."

Godfrey, Earl Inkblot cleared his throat. "But –"

"No buts, Sir Godfrey!" snapped Old Ma Knucklebone. "Just do as I say!"

Then she scooped the bones back into her pouch and held out her filthy hand.

"That'll be a sovereign, please!"

🌸 CHAPTER FOUR 🌸
Birthdays are Fun!

"Ooh! I love birthday parties!" squealed the Queen. She grabbed one of her ropes of pearls and swung it in the air like a lassoo. "What a clever idea, Godfrey!"

Godfrey, Earl Inkblot, went pink and bowed. "Thank you, Your Majesty."

"There's only one problem." The Queen's face dropped and the pearls dropped back around her neck with a clatter. "It's not my birthday."

"But it *is* Lowd Essex's birthday, Your Highness," squeaked Roderick, Lord Crusty. "We thought we could give him a surpwise."

"Ooh! I love surprises, too," cried the Queen. She jumped up from her throne and began pacing backwards and forwards. "Now, let's see, birthdays and surprises mean only one thing –"

No one spoke because no one could guess what the Queen was going to say. And if you said the wrong thing –

"A special pudding, of course!" shouted the Queen merrily. "Something the Earl of Essex would love most of all."

"On my birthday, I ordered a spun sugar pudding in the shape of my horse," cried Roderick Crusty excitedly.

He sighed and held his hands together over his heart, dramatically. "It was the best birthday ever!"

Again no one spoke. It was impossible to say whether the Queen would laugh, smile, or tip a jug of water over his head.

The Queen skipped across her chamber and held out her hand to be kissed.

"Roderick, you're a marvel!" she cried. "I shall order a Queen of Puddings! It will look just like me, be utterly wonderful and far too delicious to eat!"

Mary curtseyed. "I shall inform Toby Crumble immediately," she murmured.

"Thank you, Mary!"

Mary Marchbank nearly fell over her feet. The Queen had never thanked her in her life before!

"Now, there's just one more thing!" cried the Queen. She clapped her hands excitedly. "What shall I give him for a present?"

Matilda, Lady Mouthwater, pictured the Earl of Essex in her mind. She saw his twinkly eyes and his pink rubbery lips. She heard his false voice flattering her and the sound of his boots hammering down the corridors after her.

She shuddered and took a deep breath.

"Give Lord Essex a miniature portrait of your royal self, Majesty," said Matilda, Lady Mouthwater, sweetly. "That way, he may carry it with him wherever he goes."

"Strewth!" shouted the Queen. "What inspiration!" She jumped onto her throne and held out her arms. "Why, I believe I owe you all an apology for calling you nasty names the other day!"

There was a sharp gasp and a dull thud.

Godfrey, Earl Inkblot, fainted.

Roderick Lord Crusty turned the colour of a fish's belly.

Even Matilda, Lady Mouthwater, who was normally so cool and reserved, felt a bit woozy in the head.

As for Mary Marchbank, she had to lean on a table to get her breath back. It was completely unheard of for the Queen to apologise to anyone!

***

Robert, Earl of Essex, stood in the best room of the Essex Inn and admired himself in the mirror.

Ever since the Queen had summoned him to a birthday party in his honour, he had been convinced she would grant him his special wish.

Indeed, he had been trying to get her to agree to it these past three months. Yet while she said yes to everything else, she refused him the one thing he really wanted in the whole world.

And that was the post of Commander in her Army.

Essex grinned his ravishing grin, making his eyes light up like fireworks.

This time she wouldn't say no. Because surely no one can say no to you on your birthday? Especially if you are the Earl of Essex!

THE ESSEX ARMS

At that moment, the door opened and the Earl's manservant Walter, came into the low-timbered room.

"Are my clothes pressed and sweet-smelling, man?" demanded Essex.

Walter held out the purple satin doublet, the gold and green waistcoat embroidered with stars and the black silk breeches.

"What colour stockings would my Lord require?"

Essex thought carefully. Since purple was a royal colour, perhaps having two purple things would be overdoing it a bit.

After all, the Queen was such an old show-off herself, she didn't like show-offs around her.

"I'll wear the pure white stockings, Walter," replied the Earl of Essex.

He turned and smiled again at his reflection. "I am, after all, an unblemished character."

***

Fifteen minutes later, the Earl of Essex put on a high fancy hat with a black feather and wrapped himself in a velvet cloak.

Then, since the weather was wet and windy, he climbed into his own private coach and set off for the Queen's palace.

🏵 CHAPTER FIVE 🏵
Four Presents and a Pudding

Mary Marchbank had never seen the Queen so giddy and excited. Anyone would have thought it was her own birthday party.

All day she had fussed over the music she wanted. "I must have my choir," she demanded. "And my musicians."

She picked up a lute and plucked the strings dreamily. "And I myself shall sing a song in your

honour, my darling," she murmured, staring at the little statue of the Earl of Essex.

Mary stepped into a low curtsey. "May I enquire if Your Majesty has decided what —"

"No, you may not!" shouted the Queen. She put down the lute and stamped her foot. "We still haven't decided what we are going to wear!"

Mary turned to Matilda, Lady Mouthwater, and rolled her eyes.

What would happen if Old Ma Knucklebone was wrong? What if, after his special birthday party, Essex got everything wanted?

Matilda, Lady Mouthwater, was thinking much the same but she forced the thought from her mind.

"Her Majesty's beauty is shown best in her favourite colours of black and white," she murmured.

Lady Matilda moved over to one of the great oak chests that were lined up against the wall. Each one was full to bursting with loose dresses, petticoats, outer skirts, doublets and gowns. Each one so heavily embroidered and crusted with pearls and fine jewels that it almost stood up on its own.

She held up a particularly gorgeous black velvet gown. It had been made quite recently which meant that when the Queen wore it, it was not too tight.

Because both Mary and Lady Matilda knew that if the Queen ever insisted on wearing dresses that had fitted her when she was much younger, after a very short while, everyone paid the price.

The Queen looked closely at the velvet gown and ran her long hands over the gold embroidery that decorated the front. She held up the gauzy material, shining with pearls that floated over the shoulders like angels' wings.

"The perfect choice, Lady Matilda!" cried the Queen. "I will carry my ostrich feather fan and wear only my finest jewels."

At the other side of the room, Mary Marchbank whisked up a mixture of egg white, powdered eggshell, alum and borax. At the last minute she sprinkled on some poppy seeds and added a dash of the Queen favourite marjoram water.

Then she set aside the mixture to warm by the fire.

"Your Majesty's face preparation is ready," Mary murmured.

"Excellent!" cried the Queen. "I shall have the softest, whitest, loveliest face in the palace!

She grabbed the little statue of Essex and threw herself down in her favourite chair so that Mary could begin to apply the gloopy make-up. "Just in time for the party," she sighed to herself.

The Earl of Essex couldn't believe his eyes! He had always believed that Roderick, Lord Crusty, was a pathetic wimp.

More horse than human, in fact.

Now he was holding out a magnificent leather riding cloak and it was something that the Earl of Essex really wanted!

"For the battlefield," Lord Roderick murmured. "To protect the master and his mount."

Essex looked up in surprise. He felt moved by Lord Roderick's words. They had a certain poetry to them. He especially liked the word 'master'.

"Thank you, Lord Roderick," said Essex, smiling. "I am sure it will come in very useful."

Lord Roderick bowed. "I'm sure it will, my Lord," he replied.

Essex's twinkling eyes looked over to where the Queen was busy plucking her lute and practising the song she had promised to sing for him.

He smiled to himself. Perhaps, one day, he would be master of everything around him. After all, if you ignored the yellow wrinkly skin and the black teeth, older women did have certain qualities that younger ones lacked. Power, money and influence, for example.

Matilda, Lady Mouthwater, curtseyed. As she stared into Essex's dark shiny eyes, she made herself think of her little mongrel dog. It was the only creature in the world she had any tender feelings for at all.

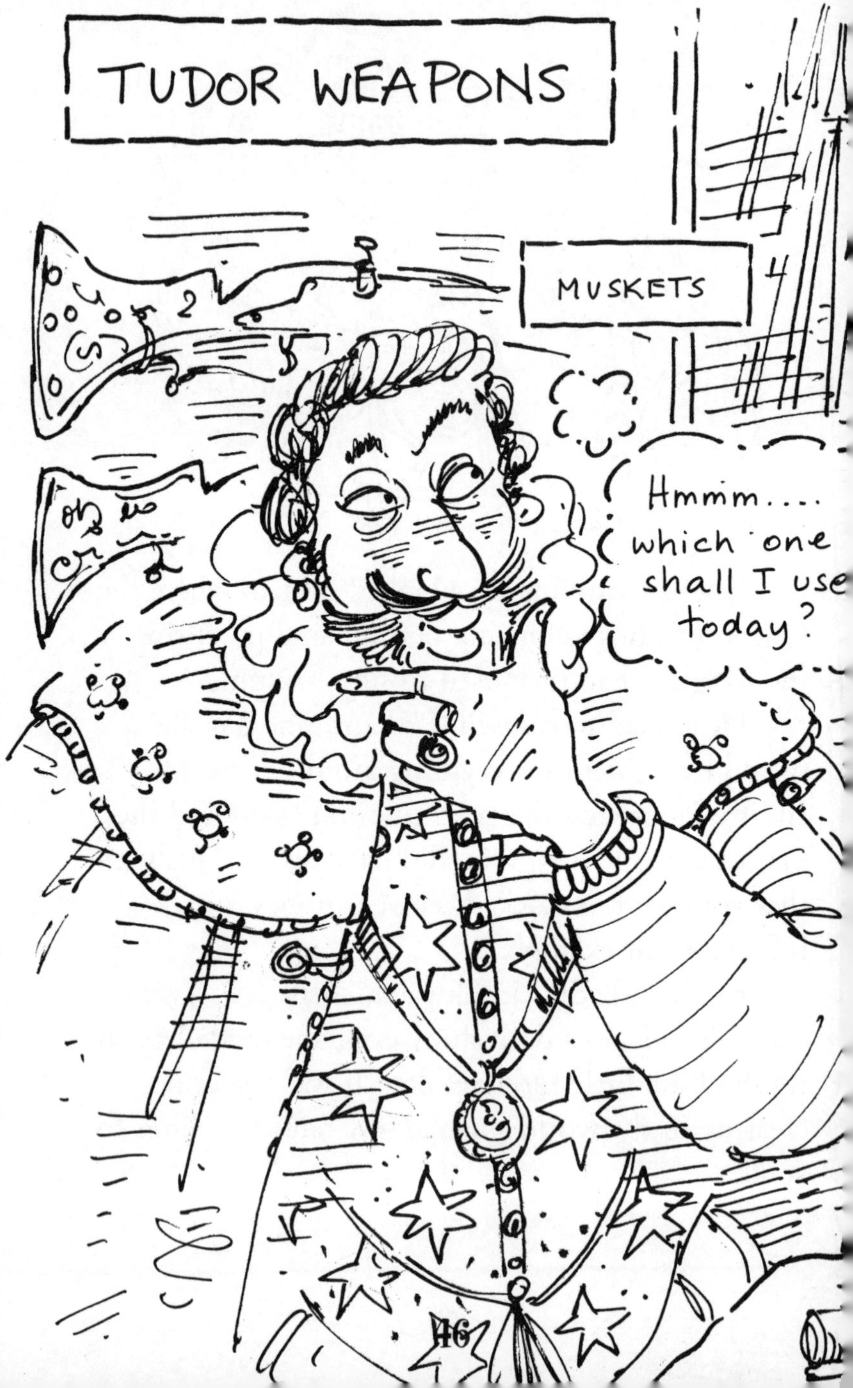
TUDOR WEAPONS
MUSKETS
Hmmm.... which one shall I use today?

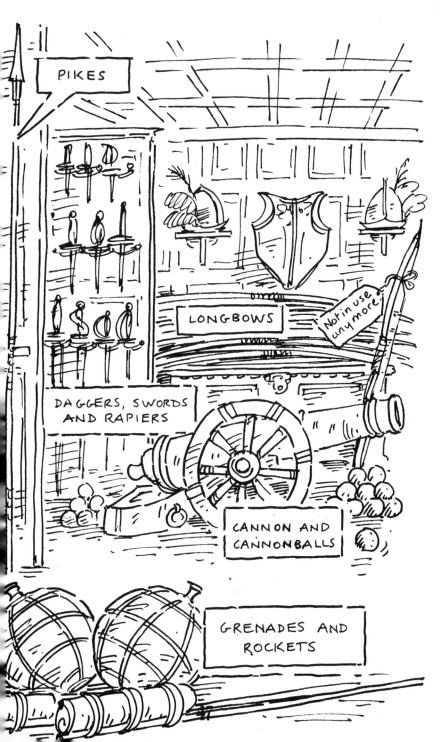

Lady Mouthwater's face softened and a smile played over her lips.

Again Essex was surprised. In the past, Matilda, Lady Mouthwater, had proved strangely immune to his charms. It had been puzzling at first, then irritating. Now, it appeared, a mist had cleared from her eyes and she, too, recognized that he was her natural master.

The Earl of Essex allowed himself a small forgiving smile in return.

"For travelling, my Lord," murmured Matilda,

Lady Mouthwater. "Lest you forget yourself."

Essex pulled away the silken wrapping. Inside was an exquisite little mirror in its own case. It was just the sort of thing a nobleman and a commander might use on a battlefield.

He picked up the mirror and

stared at his long
handsome face.
It wasn't a face that
he would ever forget.

"Thank you, Lady
Mouthwater,"
murmured the Earl
of Essex. "I will
carry it
with me on
my travels."

As he
spoke he took
her hand in his
and brought it slowly
to his lips.

Matilda, Lady Mouthwater, thought she was
going to be sick! But at the last minute, she steeled
herself and managed a curtsey before she pulled her
hand back and wiped it quickly behind her back.

At that moment, Godfrey, Earl Inkblot, placed
a portable writing table in the Earl's hands.

"With my sincerest wishes on your birthday,"
he murmured.

The Earl of Essex felt his heart leap as he
looked down at this new present.

It was the perfect choice. He always wrote his best and most charming letters from the middle of great adventures on the battlefield!

"Thank you, dear Sir," cried Essex. "This is a most precious gift indeed!"

"Not as precious as the one from me!" cried the Queen. She put down her lute and motioned Essex towards her.

Then she gave him a miniature portrait of herself. In the picture, her hair sparkled with pearls and a glittery ruff shone like a halo around a face that was young and smooth.

"To carry with you," murmured the Queen, "so that I may be with you everywhere you go."

Everywhere?

A bright white light flashed in Essex's head as he held the tiny portrait in his hand. Suddenly, he understood why all his birthday presents had something to do with travelling and going away.

The Queen was going to make him Commander in her Army. All he had to do was ask!

The Earl of Essex leaned forward, as graceful as a swan, on his bended knee.

At that moment, the door opened and Toby Crumble entered, carrying the Queen's special pudding.

CHAPTER SIX
A Terrible Temper Tantrum

Mary Marchbank gasped.

Even the Queen seemed taken aback.

As for Lady Matilda, Lord Roderick and Godfrey, Earl of Inkblot, they all stared until their eyes goggled.

A beautifully sculptured figure of the Queen, made out of spun sugar and decorated with icing jewels, rose from a purple mound of blackcurrants, raspberries and fine white cake. The mound was shaped to look like the folds of one of the Queen's royal gowns.

The figure of the Queen wore a bright red wig that rose like a sail above her head. Two curly ringlets fell, one either side of the smooth white face.

Toby Crumble had created the most magnificent pudding ever seen in the Palace.

The sugar Queen looked delicious and gorgeous all at the same time!

Only the Earl of Essex seemed unimpressed. He was too busy imagining himself on the battlefield, shouting orders and looking wonderful.

"When do I leave, Your Majesty?" he cried joyfully.

The Queen dragged her greedy eyes from the birthday pudding. There was nothing she liked better than a mouthful of yummy, sugary stuff and she had never seen so many different kinds in one place.

"I beg your pardon?" A shiver ran through the room. Everyone but the Earl of Essex heard the menace in the Queen's voice.

Essex grabbed the Queen's hand.

"When do I leave to command my own forces?"

The Queen snatched her hand back. Her eyes were hard as pellets. "What on earth are you talking about, Essex?"

Again, a shiver ran through the room. And again, everyone but the Earl of Essex heard the danger in the Queen's voice.

For a moment, Essex looked puzzled. What was going on? Was the Queen playing a little game with him before she gave him his birthday wish?

"I shall write to you every day, Your Majesty," cried the Earl of Essex with a voice as smooth as treacle. "I shall ride into battle with your beloved portrait next to my heart."

The Queen stood up. "You'll do no such thing!" she snapped. "Since when have I made you a Commander in my Army?"

The Earl of Essex stared at the Queen with his mouth open. Why was she insisting on playing this silly game? Perhaps it was time he spoke to her plainly?

"It is my birthday wish to be made Commander in your Army, Your Majesty," he cried. "Have you not granted it to me?"

"I most certainly have not!" shouted the Queen. "Whoever heard of such nonsense?"

She smirked and picked up her lute. "You are to stay here with me and listen to my song."

The bright white light in the Earl's head exploded and shattered into a thousand pieces.

"But it's my birthday!" he shouted. "And I want to be a Commander in your Army."

"How dare you speak to me like that," cried the Queen. She threw the lute across the room. "Who do you think you are?"

At that moment, two things happened.

First, the musicians on the other side of the room became so frightened, they started to play a soppy old-fashioned tune called 'Lime Stockings'. It was one of the Queen's favourites and the Earl of Essex hated it. And second, the Earl of Essex completely lost his temper.

Before he knew what he was doing,

he had picked up the Queen's special birthday pudding, thrown it on the floor and stamped on it.

Bits of sloppy cake and blackcurrant flew everywhere.

"I want to be a Commander!" bellowed the Earl of Essex.

"No!" shrieked the Queen, as a piece of purple pudding dribbled down her face.

"Yes!" screamed the Earl of Essex. Then in a fit of rage he picked up the portable desk and the mirror and smashed them both on the floor.

Mary Marchbank had just enough time to grab the Queen's portrait before the Earl turned and stomped towards the door.

"You will NOT turn your back on me!" yelled the Queen. She held up her arm and pointed one long finger at the Earl. "Say you're sorry or I'll have your head chopped off!"

Something in the Queen's voice made the Earl of Essex stop in his tracks and turn around.

"Sorry," he muttered.

"I should think so, too!" cried the Queen. She lifted herself up to her full height. "You are banished from my Court!"

The colour drained from the Earl of Essex's face. It wasn't supposed to happen like this. It was his birthday. What had gone wrong?

Then, something in the look on the faces of Mary Marchbank, Lady Matilda Mouthwater, Lord Rockerick and Godfrey, Earl of Inkblot made his stomach turn.

Somehow, and in a way he didn't quite understand, the Earl of Essex knew he had been framed!

***

Mary Marchbank set a jug of steaming marjoram water on the table beside the Queen's chair.

In front of her, the Queen sat on her throne with her head resting back on a small velvet cushion. The red wig was gone and her long, wispy grey hair lay in strands around her old, tired face.

"I shall miss the Earl of Essex," murmured the Queen drowsily. "Even though he is a spoiled brat, he made me laugh."

She reached out towards the tiny statue he had given her. But the cuff of her sleeve caught the edge of the table and statue fell onto the floor. The two women watched as the head broke off and slowly rolled across the oak floor boards.

The Queen sighed. "That's what will happen to that spoilt brat if he doesn't learn to behave."

And suddenly she looked older and tired than ever before.

Mary Marchbank said nothing. Indeed there was nothing to say.

She picked up the Queen's hairbrush and began to brush her long grey hair.

✿ NOTES ✿
At the Court of Queen Elizabeth
(How it really was!)

The Earl of Essex

The Earl of Essex was thirty-three years younger than the Queen. He was handsome, clever and ambitious. The Queen was obsessed with him and gave him almost everything he wanted. She even made him a Commander in her Army in Ireland.

But Essex was arrogant and reckless and refused to follow orders. When the Queen finally cut off his money, Essex led a rebellion against her. He was beheaded in 1601.

The Queen never recovered and kept his portrait with her until she died two years later.

Tudor Inns and Coaches

A network of inns criss-crossed England in Tudor times. Foreign visitors praised their high standards, comfort and cleanliness. The inns served as stopping places for coaches, where fresh horses could be obtained.

Coaches had only recently arrived in England from Germany but they had no springs and were extremely uncomfortable to travel in.

The roads themselves were no more than dirt tracks and in bad weather the coaches often got stuck in boggy mud.

Tudor Furniture

Tudor furniture was elaborately carved and often inlaid with other woods. Oak was the most commonly used wood. Houses were still sparsely furnished at this time, but wealthy tradesmen men had chests, stools and tables. Only very rich people had chairs and beds.

The Queen herself commissioned a number of superbly carved four poster beds and she never travelled anywhere without one.

Musical Instruments

The Queen was an acomplished musician. She could play the lute, the lyre and a keyboard instrument called the virginals. Her court singers and players were famous all over Europe for the quality of their music. She had a choir of fifty people and over forty musicians.
The Queen also composed music and ballets.

Tudor Weapons

During the reign of Queen Elizabeth I, the longbow finally gave way to firearms. However, early muskets were heavy and unreliable. They needed a flask or waterproof pouch of gunpowder, a bag of bullets, several yards of wadding paper and a flint for lighting the match. All these were slung around the soldier's waist. Gunpowder was also used in grenades which exploded into lethal fragments of iron.